I0829588

Nellie the War Chick

"A purpose filled life."

The most basic question everyone
faces in life is why am I here?

Find something more important than
you are and dedicate your life to it.

Illustrated and written by
Gregory G. Newson

Based on David Chaltas story

Published by Newson Publishing
Newburgh, New York

Author and Illustrator: Gregory G. Newson

ACKNOWLEDGMENTS

David Chaltas

Michael Wade

All inquiries should be addressed to;

Newson Publishing, P.O.Box 53, Newburgh, NY 12551

Https://www.NewsonPublishing.com

ISBN: 978-0-578-63267-4

History is replete with many stories of how influential chickens are in human society. The Romans were among those who first used the chickens to predict the future. In one radio interview with an author who has written books on the history of chicken's powerful roles in society, the writer pointed out that the Roman military once used chickens to consider whether or not to wage war on their enemies. Then, any military general who did not consult a fowl before making military decisions was considered incompetent and stupid.

Apart from the military, the Senate also relied on sacred chickens for auguries. They used the behavior of the sacred chicken to draw conclusions on national issues. If the sacred chicken consumed the grains presented, they assumed that the omen was favorable. If it does not eat the grain, they presumed that the augury was unfavorable.

They depended on this system so much because they believed sacred chickens possessed some supernatural powers that made them intelligent, smart, courageous, and shrewd. This information made me wonder whether Lee was also privy to the inner thoughts of the Romans, who used chickens to make military decisions.

According to legend, Western civilization would have been extinct if chickens had not inspired the Greek army to defeat the Persian army. On his way to attack the intruding Persian troops, the Athenian general Themistocles saw two cocks fighting. He intervened: "Behold, these do not fight for their household gods, for the monuments of their ancestors, for glory, for liberty or the safety of their children, but only because one will not give way to the other." Although no one knows how the fight ended, it was believed that the bout inspired the Greek soldiers to defeat their enemies.

DEDICATION

I am dedicating this book to all those who have owned a beloved pet, including those who understand the meaning of the unconditional love which animals have for their owners.

To General Maggie Sue's family and my belove Lisa Blanding who soon will become my wife, my grandchildren and those who are endeared to me, I offer this book with love.

3

In this book, the author me; Gregory Newson set out to tell a historical correct fact and present it from the perspective of a hen that was present when America was at a pivotal point in its fledgling history. By reading this book, you will become immersed in the story of how Nellie distinguished herself from other chickens.

ABOUT THE BOOK

The story of Nellie is based on a historical account of a pet owned by Robert E.Lee, an American soldier who commanded the Confederate States Army during the American Civil War. Lee rescued the little hen and provided a refuge for the animal in his camp. This book takes the reader on a journey, from the farm where Nellie was hatched to the point where the general befriended her and later granted the bird amnesty. This book also explores the hen's expedition as she witnesses the ravages of war and tries to make sense out of the needless bloodshed caused by the "upright walker" creatures. The saga of Nellie is presented from her perspective, thus offering readers more insight into what she witnessed during the American Civil War.

A SPRING CHICKEN

My name is Nellie, a small black hen. I guess you could say I am the luckiest chicken in the world. Well, I think being lucky was my destiny. I believe that everyone has a destiny and that it falls upon every creature to find that purpose and embrace it. Unlike many animals, I found my purpose in life unexpectedly.

So, who is Nellie? I was what you call a spring chicken. I was hatched on a farm in the northern Virginia area when the yellow lilies bloomed. I am not sure of the name of the farm or its owner. I can still recall what mother said about Hamilton's Crossing, but I am not sure what that means anyway.

Let me also tell you a few things about my family. My mother was a beautiful black hen, and my father's main body was covered with black and white speckled feathers. Besides having spurs that seemed to be larger than life, my dad was the cock of the barnyard and chicken coop.

I was not the only child. I had several brothers and sisters, and our parents loved us dearly. However, my mum was quite protective of her kids. I remember scampering around, while my mother was clucking and warning us to be wary of intruders. She always hovered over us and watched our every move. She wouldn't even let the old farmer get too close to us. If he tried to move closer to us, she would warn him by clucking frantically and spreading her wings. And if he ventured too close to us, she would deal with him severely!

Most barnyard animals respected my mother, as well. I remember when the farmer's dog encroached on our lot and tried to chase some of us away. My mother came clucking and running; she laid a good flogging on that old hound dog. The dog took off howling and eventually had his tail between his legs.

My mum's concern for us was never-ending. In fact, the older we were, the more my mother seemed to worry about our safety. She would call us and cluck to us. At night, she would tuck us under her wings and protect us not only from the cold weather but also from any creatures that attempted to grab one of her ba-

bies. I also remember waking up to the sound of a "hoot." Although I was scared, my mother pampered me, clucking softly to assure me everything was fine.

The next morning, my mother tried to explain what happened the previous night to us. She told us that the old farmer must have scared off the big-eyed bird and that the farmer was our protector. Little did she realize that he was also our enemy. Over time, I noticed that occasionally, one of my fellow birds would be missing. It happened every time the farmer's wife came out to the barnyard. She would chase us until she caught one of us, and then she would go behind the woodshed to slaughter the bird. I complained to my parents about this practice. But my father said she was freeing that bird and fulfilling its purpose. I never fully understood what he meant then until I became an adult hen.

Growing up came with more responsibility. When I was as a baby hen, no one ever chased me. But as I grew older, my daddy would say, "Exercise and work on your speed and dodging skills, as these are your survival tools." I listened to his advice: I got so fast that I barely noticed my feet on the ground when I am running. My pace allowed me to dodge and zigzag so efficiently that the famer's wife didn't want to waste her time chasing me anymore.

Whenever she came into the barnyard, I would run. I became remarkably good at dodging her. Sometimes, by luck, she would get close to me, and I would quickly change my direction. At times, I would run right threw her legs. However, she caught my sister and a couple of my brothers. I thought perhaps she might have set them free because I never saw them again after that incidence.

I also remember when my father fought with a new rooster over territory and wives. It was a Pyrrhic victory, however. My father was badly injured from the spurs of that old red rooster, even though he won the bout. The next morning, the farmer's spouse chased and caught my father and the old rooster. My father protested, but his effort was ineffective: He was taken out behind the woodshed along with the old red rooster. I heard my father yell something, but I couldn't make anything out of his speech. I always wanted to think he was telling me goodbye after I noticed some red feathers along with the speckled ones floating in the wind that afternoon. I knew the speckled feathers were from my father. I guessed he was molting. After dad's disappearance, my mother told me that my older brother would be the "king" around the barnyard henceforth.

It took me a while to digest the fact that my dad was gone forever. I remember the wind getting cold and white flakes falling. One spring, however, things changed around the farm. The farmer's wife cried after she saw her children carrying those fire sticks. I felt sorry for her, nonetheless. I guess they were going to find freedom too. The farm's routine became monotonous except for the day the farmer's wife chased and caught my mother. I remember her distressed call. I also remember how other chickens shrieked at the top of their lungs when they saw her in captivity. Distraught, I watched as she took her behind the shed. It was on that day that I felt the taste of hate. I knew then that I must never allow any of those strange beings to catch me. The only thing that consumed my thought was how to escape from the barnyard. Unbeknown to me, that day was around the corner.

THE GRAY-HAIRED ONE

One day, the ambiance of our peaceful valley suddenly became

different.

All the farm animals could perceive the drastic changes in the wind. The sky was free from clouds, yet booms of thunder sounded from a distance.

The air was also undeniably filled with the scent of upright crea- tures and sulfur. At times, the ground shook under our feet. Everyone, including the farmers, was scared.

On a very chilly fall morning, a year after I was born in early 1862, a whole bunch of upright walker creatures dressed in gray and butternut colored uniform marched onto our Virginia farm. They carried sticks on their shoulders while motioning toward out territory.

As they moved closer to the yard, all the hens started clucking with nervous excitement and checking on their chicks. The farm owners wasted no time in greeting them when they arrived in our compound. The way they treated the troops was quite unusual. They welcomed them courteously and poured some beer into their cups.

The farmer's wife first served the drink to a pale white hairy up- right-walking man who had a shiny metal insignia on his coat. After they finished the drink, they all began to smile and share kind words. Then, suddenly, they started pointing fingers at us and marching with large bags in their hands in our direction. In less than two minutes, a few of them in strange butternut clothing captured the horses. They also took the old milk cow and the mean old Billy goat who didn't have many friends. I was glad to see him taken away, however.

What happened on that day was unprecedented. In the past, captors only chased and caught only one chicken, which was then carried behind the shed.

But this time, with the support of other upright-walking creatures, the farmer and his wife rushed into the yard. They closed the yard door and started catching all the animals one by one. Next, they tied their legs together and threw them into a brown bag that contained the feed. Determined not to be caught, I ran as fast as I could. But in the end, I was caught. Afterward, my legs were tied with thick ropes before they placed me inside that dark bag. The bag we were in was thrown onto the back of a wagon, thereby exposing us to excruciating heat.

Staying inside the bag was stressful. As about ten of us were crammed inside that burlap bag, I struggled to breathe. I couldn't fathom why they treated us like that after feeding us for so long. I saw my younger sister at the bottom of the bag. She was looking tensed. I tried to comfort her, but the situation at hand was just too much for all of us. I became so thirsty for the first time in my life that I experienced hunger.

While the wagon was moving, I thought to myself what would be- come of the flock. A few hours later, the wagon stopped, and I heard many people talking. I could recognize their voices. I knew we were completely surrounded by the same intruders who cap- tured us behind the woodshed. This made me figured out what I had to do.

Immediately the bag opened, and some of my relatives were yanked out by their feet. I heard them protesting before I felt an eerie silence. I was tied to an older hen who protested when they pulled us out by the string. She cackled at the top of her lungs and tried to fly away. Her effort didn't deter the captors. They wrung her neck. I was horrified when I saw what they did. Imme-

diately one of the creatures cut the rope holding us together, I dashed out of the upright grip.

One person tried to grab my neck, but I was too fast for him. Unfazed, those creatures dressed in gray outfits tried to catch me. I applied all the tricks that I had learned from being chased by the farmer's spouse, so I was able to out-run them. But I knew I had to hide. So, I waited until only a few of the younger ones chased me before running into a thicket. They followed me persistently. As they looked for me in the under-growth, I slipped away.

I noted a strange object, which had cloth flaps on it, sticking up in the air. I ran inside and hid under a material that was off the ground, but it had something like the items worn by those chas-ing me. The only difference was that the material was covering a long object with the wool hanging over it. I was glad because I could hide under it without being noticed.

For some reason, they gave up searching for me. I didn't know how long I stayed there, but the urge to lay an egg hit me. As the ground was too hard to lay the egg, I slowly peeped out from under the item hanging down and began to explore. I noticed that I could fly on top of my hiding place. In fact, the place resembled my nest in the hen house. So, I settled down to lay my egg.

As I felt the egg leaving my body, I gave out a cackle by reflex. Immediately I realized that I had given them a clue of where I

was, I knew I was in trouble. The flaps opened, and I saw the same person one who drank the black stuff the farmer's wife gave him. He was standing at the entrance. Scared to death, I backed away from the shadow's edge. I noticed that the white-haired one was coming through the flap while another person fol-lowed him closely from behind.

"You may leave me now, Bill my thanks for your company." "'Yes-sir Marsa Lee." I thought he was following the instructions of the white creature. I heard some pockets of noise outside the tent. So, I thought it was safe to stick my head out a little. I saw the black creature with the person who had gray hair on his head and beards leave. I watched him closely, observing how he stood before a mirror and removed parts of his body. First, he peeled away the gray cloth that covered his body with shiny gold spots. Next, he removed the next layer of material. I waited for him to finish undressing. However, it was this small yet careless period of waiting that allowed him to see me through the mirror, which he was standing in front of. I peeked out from under his thing, which he called his bed. He moved closer to me and introduced himself. " Hi, my name is Robert Lee," he said, "and that's my bed and what's yours." "Ha Ha," he chuckled, "I know I'm going to name you Nellie."

Then the gray-haired headed one called out: "Bill, Bill come. I need you to look closely at our new friend." The cook Bill replied, "Marsa that's no chicken; that's a hen." They later found my egg. I heard them talking about the egg, but I couldn't understand what they were saying. The gray-haired headed one was fondling, turning and marveling at the egg, as though it was the most interesting thing in the world. Seeing him excited about my egg, I felt a little bit proud of producing something so interesting,

But the white-headed upright creature didn't move towards me. In fact, he stepped away from me. He turned to Bill and pointed his finger in the direction of the nest outside. After that, Bill

dashed to the front of the tent to a big wagon and brought back something I was familiar with. The gray-haired one gently tossed some of the golden sunshine, which my mother called corn, on the floor and then quietly stood still.

I was scared to eat at first, but my hunger overcame my fear. I ate until I felt I was going to bust. Hearing other upright creatures approaching, I flew to the highest perch I could find in the tent. Slowly the gray-haired one opened the flap and pushed a can filled with water towards me. Again, he smiled and called to me. "Here chick, chick, chick," he said as he crumbled some cornbread down close to the water. He then backed off and left me alone.

The gray-haired one fed me like this several times in a day for more than two weeks. Over time, I slowly I realized that he would not hurt me. Besides he knew how to say these magic words: "Here chick, chick, chick." And I knew what that meant. By the end of some days, I allowed him to visit the shelter without cackling or complaining.

Leaving the nests always left me extremely stressed and tired. But as darkness approached, I would find a perch. And to my surprise, he always removed my egg and slept beside me.

Over time, I was not afraid of him anymore. He was different from the farmers. He seemed so kind and nice to me. Any time he wanted to feed me, he kept saying the magic words that always produced food and then ended the statement with "Nellie." He also called me "hen." For some reasons, I trusted this gray-haired one more than others whom I had ever known.

Within a couple of days, I followed him around as though he was my mother. He always had a treat for me in his pocket, and his voice was so soothing to my ears. When he talked to the other creatures, they all listened. Based on this, I assumed he was the head rooster. When he was talking to others, he used the word "amnesty." I never understood the meaning, but I knew the term applied to me. Whatever it meant, I was quite sure I had free reign over the whole place.

I became so comfortable that even the cooks made a special place for me to lay my egg. I also got so used to traveling that every morning after my treats, I would listen to the gray-haired one to say, "Strike the tents," and then I would go to the old pot that hung down from one of the wagons. My nests were also attractive: They were filled with straw. As I traveled, I would lay an egg. Whenever I cackled, the cook would attend to my needs, fixing my egg for the gray-haired one. I felt that was the least I could do for him for saving my life.

Many times, I would strut around the camps, and the ones who followed the gray-haired one would say, "There's little Nellie, the general's chicken." I would advertise myself, pushing my chest out and displaying my spectacular feathers. The upright creatures would have little bits of hardtack for me. I resent eating it because they didn't have much quantity. Like me, they loved the gray-haired one, and they liked anything he loved.

Besides, every upright walker creature seemed to admire him. Because of his prestige, they respected me too. No matter where I went, the cooks gave me food and pampered me like a toddler. I was always pecking the ground around their wagons because they dropped crumbs for me. They always talked to me and called me Nellie or just "hen." Bill, who was the cook for the gray-haired one, was treated like the general's kin. I also noticed that those upright walkers had a lot of respect for one another. I was

HUMMEL
COFFEE
BORDEN'S
LECHE
VAPORADA

blessed to be guarded by them, including others within the camp.

The new-found experience reminded me of home, where we all looked out for each other even if the intruders were cows, horses, ducks, sheep, or chickens.

THE COOK AND BODY SERVANT

I became quite fond of all the servants. The color of my feathers was the same as their skin. A few of them had the same name as their masters. Later, I found that many of them were raised by their master ancestors before the kinsmen began fighting each other. Bill would talk to me as I ran around, eating castoff scraps. I can still recall the odors of food being cooked. Those upright walker cooks could fix a meal out of anything. But everyone bragged about Bill's cooking.

THE LONG MARCH
Lord knows I have more experience than other chickens. I have been to so many places, and I have seen many unimaginable things. The thunder elicited from those men's fire sticks made me wonder what could have happened to my home. Sometimes, I wondered what my goal on earth was. After all, I didn't have any chicks to protect and care for.

I married the big red rooster on the farm, but he later went behind the woodshed and never returned. Perhaps he ran off with another pullet. The only thing I did was traveling with the gray-haired one from one place to the other. Even though I supplied him an egg every day, I felt my effort was not enough. Maybe someday, I could render more service to him and put a smile on his face.

I did not like to see him upset, but he seemed so sad at times. In the tent, I had caught him many times on his knees, praying and crying. During our travels, I saw the destruction of many buildings, animals, upright walkers, and properties. Sometimes, the thunder was so loud that I couldn't hear my own cackle when I laid an egg. But when the gray-haired one came and interacted with me, I felt calmer. I must admit: He had a unique way of making me elated.

The other creatures were always saluting him, but he tried not to disturb them. I had seen him sleeping outside of his nest because one of the younger upright walkers was sleeping there.

The rumor around the corral was that the gray-haired one received a bunch of talking leaves, one of which contained information about his daughter's demise. After reading the leaf, he gently placed it back in his pocket and then took care of the needs of all the other upright walkers. My mind was filled with pride due to his display of equanimity. My master learned that his daughter was dead, yet he took care of the needs of others before being overcome with grief. I vowed on that day I would sacrifice my life for him if needed.

Early that morning, the gray-haired one gave his usual order of "Strike the tents." I had no choice but to go to my tent. All what we did was to stay on the road. Later, I got so bored sitting in the wagon or riding in the bucket laying eggs that I wanted to get out and stretch my legs. After we stopped occasionally, the cook gave me food. However, I was not hungry most times. We kept navigating away from my home, and I couldn't help but noticed that most of the upright walkers were tired and couldn't walk well.

They needed something to protect their feet during the journey.

Nonetheless, the routine was always the same. We would wake up early, break camp, and begin marching. The roads had deep marks on the earth from the wagons, and the dust was terrible. Sometimes, when the sky shed tears, the roads would be muddy and difficult to navigate. At times, we had to build a platform to cross the rivers.

Occasionally, I would wrap my head under my wing and sleep off. When we halted to rest the horses, they would graze on whatever they could find, and the cooks were always looking for food. In fact, they had some of those upright walkers doing what was called foraging. I don't know how they captured prey like cows and pigs. But when they came back, they had something to eat. But the numbers of the hunted game declined over time.

I was nonetheless so proud to observe how those upright walkers living on their farms addressed my master with deference. I heard one say, "I wish he was ours." But I didn't know what she was talking about. One even asked him to write his name on the talking leaf. I didn't understand the benefit of such gesture anyway. Sometimes those upright walkers didn't make much sense to me.

Our journey seemed never-ending. I thought we were on the move forever, but finally we reached a place named Cashtown. This small town was in Pennsylvania, a place where I had never heard animals talking before. The gray-haired one went inside one of the houses in the town. The building was like a beehive. Those upright walkers in gray went back and forth to the structure. However, I wanted them to leave my master alone.

I knew he was sick because he didn't eat all the eggs I laid for him. He looked pale and had to excuse himself often. But when he came back, he looked so exhausted and tired. I pleaded with my clucks for him to rest. He wasn't listening to me. He would go somewhere and "take a knee." At times, he said, "St Andrew's please deliver me." I didn't know what good that would do, but he came back looking somewhat better.

WHEN THE EARTH SHOOK

I recall seeing the earth shaking and hearing the thunder from a distance. I thought to myself that the world was about to end. No pecking order was observed between the upright walkers in gray and those in blue. I predicted that they were trying to establish which group was more superior. I remember seeing my master on his horse named Traveller. He kept looking in the direction of the thunder and asking what was happening.

I beckoned to Traveller, inquiring about what was happening. He replied that a fight

over shoes was going on at a place called Gettysburg. Traveller nevertheless assured me that our current paths would lead us to the destination. He also advised me to stay close to the wagon and try not to follow our master.

Our journey to Gettysburg was a new experience for me. I had never felt the ground tremble vigorously like that before. The closer we were to the battleground, the more I felt the ground shaking uncontrollably. Many creatures were running away from the town as though foxes were hunting chickens. The blue ones and the gray ones were fighting in the streets.

The gray-haired one set up camp at Ms. Mary Thompson's house and made most of his upright walkers travel along a ridge, popularly known as Seminary Ridge. The men in blue were on another ridge called Cemetery Ridge. Another chicken said that one ridge dealt with life and the other dealt with death. I didn't realize exactly what that meant until a few days later.

Throughout the day, the ground shook and thunder roared. I heard screams of pain from a distance. When I moved closer, I saw many wounded upright walkers on the ground. One of the horses without an upright walker on his back galloped by and yelled that they were killing horses, mules, cows, pigs, and chickens. That alarm sent a shiver down my neck. I huddled in my tent. Nevertheless, I performed my duty by laying an egg for my gray-haired master.

That evening, the gray-haired one came to my camp. I allowed him to pick me up. He stroked my feathers and offered me some corn. I wish he could hear me so that I could tell him I left an egg for him in the tent. I also wanted to let him know how proud I was to be his hen. I think somehow, he understood my feelings. He carried me over to a corral and gave all the horses an apple. His gesture did not surprise me anymore. He showed natural care for animals. And we animals adored him.

We went back to the camp, and he tucked me in my tents. I heard sobs from his resting place that night. There was an uneasiness amongst the camp that I couldn't explain. The following morning an eerie silence quieted the sounds of battle. Once in a while, I heard the sound of wagons going up and down the hill. A rumor was passed that the injured ones were going home in wagons. I began to think how strange the war was: Sometimes, they were killing each other; At times, they were trying to save the ones whom they were trying to kill. I couldn't understand the rationale behind their seemingly contradictory actions.

A few hours later, rain fell, and the ground became muddy. The gray-haired one met with others, and they seemed to act like they expected the upright walkers in blue to attack the enemies. To be honest, I think both sides were worn to a frazzle. I was concerned about only one person – my owner. I tried to stay closer to him, but I was shooed away by those around him.

That evening, the upright walkers in gray began preparation to dispatch. I knew we would once again be leaving our area and going somewhere else. I imagined the creates staging another fight. Those upright walkers couldn't or wouldn't give up.

By chance, I saw my master again. He was staring into the distance. But I knew he was trying to figure out how to get to those upright walkers in blue. Slowly the wind became friendlier, and I knew a change was about to occur. Little did I realize just how

big the change would be. It was then that I realized my calling, my purpose, and my destiny. I figured out what I had to do.

I started walking around the cook, much to his annoyance. On one occasion, he shooed me away. Unfazed, I kept pestering him. I cackled and made such a ruckus that he finally picked me up and started to place me under a bucket. His eyes met mine. And for a moment, we simply stared at each other. I nodded, but I don't think he understood my gesture. For a few moments, he held me and stroked my feathers passionately. Then he picked up a long stick with a sharp piece of iron and headed towards the back of the chuck wagon. He stopped and looked at me one more time.

I saw drops of water falling from his eyes. I clucked to encourage him. We stepped behind the wagon. At that moment, I realized what the farm woman had to do when she took my kinfolk behind the woodshed. At last, I repaid my debt to the gray-haired one.

RELEVANT SOURCES

Poetry of the Civil War: Poems for a Bygone Era; Chaltas, David; Copyrighted; 2006

R.E. Lee: A Biography; Freeman, Douglas Southall; New York; Charles Scribner's Sons; 1934

Life & Letters of Gen. Robert Edward Lee; Jones, W.J.; Sprinkle Publications; Harrisonburg, Virginia; 1986; @ by Neale Publishing Company in 1906

The Wartime Papers of Robert E. Lee; Dowdey, Clifford and Manarin, Louis H.; De Capo Press; Commonwealth of Virginia; 1961

Grey Fox: Robert E. Lee and the Civil War; Davis, Burke; Wings Books, an imprint of Random House Value Publishing; New York; 1956; pages 51-60

Fading of the Grey; Chaltas, David; 2001

https://h2g2.com/entry/A87801546
https://civilwartalk.com/threads/war-chicken.89434/
https://emergingcivilwar.com/2012/02/20/war-chicken/
https://www.americancivilwarforum.com/what-was-the-name-of-general-robert-e.-lees-pet-chicken-who-laid-eggs-under-his-cot-every-day-32021.html

Historical Fact: General Lee's "Nellie" demise can at the "Battle of the Wilderness," Lee had invited several Generals to dine with him and his cook couldn't find sufficient food to accommodate all of General Lee's guests, so he killed "Nellie" and served her as part of Lee's dinner party.

Apparently General Lee was less than happy to find out what had happed to his "little black hen," and profusely scolded his cook, William Mack Lee for taking such actions.